Daddy Teaching Sex

Forbidden Explicit Rough Hottest Taboo Erotic Sexy

Short Stories For Adults

Lana Kendra

it wasn't bought for your personal use only, go back to

your favorite ebook retailer and buy your copy. Thank you

for acknowledging this author's efforts.

Table of Contents

Content Warning

Due to its sexual content, this book is only for those over the age of legal adulthood. There are some topics with a lot of foul language. All of the characters are at least eighteen years old.

Introduction

Are you in search of an exciting and thrilling book to read? Look no further than this extensive collection of Erotic Suspense book. I offer a wide range of genres, including Romantic Erotica, Fantasy, and Urban BDSM Fiction, to cater to even the most discerning reader. Whether you enjoy Anthologies, Westerns, or Paranormal Romance, I have something to suit your taste. My collection also includes Poetic Folklore, Interracial, Black & African American Literary Criticism, and Gothic Horror for those who crave a deeper and darker reading experience. If you're interested in Futuristic, LGBTQ+, Short Stories, or Lesbian literature, my diverse range of options will keep you captivated. Additionally, I offer Humorous, Victorian, New Adult, and College Women's Psychological Mysteries for those seeking a lighter but equally engaging read. Furthermore, My Fairy Tale Collections,

Transgender, Contemporary Western, Bisexual, and Poetry genres will transport you to different worlds and explore a variety of themes. For my Teen and Young Adult readers, I have a selection of European Geography, Cultures, eBooks, Loners, Outcasts, Mythology, Folk Tales, and much more. With such a wide array of options to choose from, you'll never run out of thrilling and enchanting stories to immerse yourself in.

It is important to emphasize that this content is exclusively intended for individuals who are 18 years of age or older.

Daddy Teaching Sex

"Honey, they canceled all the flights back home in advance."

Yes, that is what I heard on the news. This storm is really intense. It's hard to think that it's 80 degrees now and that the high will be minus 10 tomorrow.

I've heard that once the rain comes, everything will ice over. They said that it will resemble building ice layers in a backyard rink using a water hose.

"They are already getting ready here in D.C. for our governor to declare a disaster."

"They just did a governor interview on TV," I said. Nobody will lose power, he claimed. Our power system is prepared for any situation. As he puts it.

"Jason, I have concerns regarding April." That flat has no insulation at all and paper-thin walls. It's all electric, too.

She'll be stuck if the electricity goes out. Our backup generator is here. She must remain with you until this storm passes, at least for tonight.

Even though we heat with gas, we still use electricity to run the air conditioner, refrigerator, internet, and some lights. The generator has the capacity to provide all of those essential electrical requirements.

I'll give her a call to inform her. Is she working till six?"

April and I are as much of a family as we are. I'm more popular with her than my own daughter is.

Yes, but if her office doesn't close early, please tell her to leave early. The storm will intensify by six. Jason, I'm very concerned. This snow storm is reportedly the best one ever recorded.

I understand, Jennifer. I'll give her a call and make plans to come get her. I'll test the generator after that. A month has passed since the previous test.

"Nice concept... How about Brandi, Jason?"

My child. She resides in the same building of apartments.

I detest my guts, Brandi. My 'compromising' posture with her best friend Marilyn led to the divorce. During my year-long affair with her, I became negligent. The split happened quickly.

I simply can't resist touching the young women. Marilyn was the greatest, not the first. a lot more fervent than my former spouse. My thoughts turned to all of our crazy sex encounters. Superb blowjobs ever. Well, anything. no longer.

"I'll give it my best shot, but I doubt she'll want my assistance."

"April and her are buds; have her talk to her."

"Excellent idea, but let me try first."

I have to give it my all. I hope she'll forgive me someday.

I love it when she calls me "Dad."

Hello, April! Mom said you should stay with me while we weather the storm.

"All right, when can you come get me at the apartment?" In this manner, my vehicle will remain in the garage and out of the storm.

Yes, without a doubt. When is it?"

"They are releasing us at five." Six would do? I need some time to get ready, take care of some things, and prepare my suitcase.

Sounds fine. Hey, I'm going to give Brandi a call and invite her to come along.

Dear Dad... You are aware of her next move.

Yes, like when hell freezes over or go bleep yourself, I replied.

So true, she laughed.

"Mom advised you to call and persuade her."

Yes, I'll give her a call.

Can you take credit for the idea?"

"Certainly, but I don't think it will matter."

Tell me, please. See ya at six.

It's been a while since I saw Brandi, so I hope April is successful.

I gave the generator a test. Exactly! performed faultlessly.

Next, I gave the fireplaces that ran on natural gas a test. The living room would not start, darn it. It's the switch, in my opinion. I made few calls to locate one. Either out of stock or required a 1-2 day delivery time from their warehouse to me or the store. Not really necessary with the generator.

The fireplace in the master bedroom operated perfectly.

Here we go. Drive to April for 30 minutes.

I tapped. No response. Time and time again. I expected the door to be locked when I tested it. The key I possess is unlocked. I should give her a lesson on that. In the same complex, there had been a rape and severe beating just the week before.

In the kitchen and living room, I didn't see her. In the bedroom, of course. A worry-lightening bolt struck me. I had to look in the bedroom.

May I? April, huh? April, huh?"

Not a reply. There was an open bedroom door. Not in April. The bathroom door to the suite closed. I tapped.

May I? April, it's Dad here.

Not a reply.

I let the door open.

She was there, taking a shower while nude. Suds all over her body. She was rinsing off the soap slowly with the shower head that detaches.

She twiddled the shower head over her breasts, her nipples taut from her manipulation. The water splattering on them and trickling across her pubic hair and down to her firm tummy.

I ought to go now. She's alright. Indeed, I ought to go.

I find it difficult to leave.

I found myself both captivated and aroused by this sensual scene. Two weeks have passed since the last sex.

I had to find out what came next. I reached down into my training shorts and pulled my protruding penis out.

How am I acting? I reinserted it. If she turned to face me, she could notice it.

That might not be a bad thing. Give it up! She's the stepdaughter of you.

She shifted the head to her back and then to her firmly formed cheeks. She surprised me by spreading her legs and putting the shower head right on her pussy from behind.

She gripped her breasts, again twitching the nipples, and closed her eyes, keeping the head pressed firmly against her pussy.

With closed eyes, she turned to face the glass door. She was speaking in a whisper. I heard fragments.

True enough... Oh, exactly like that. Fuck me, please (incoherently). I need it badly, deep inside.

Keeping herself steady, she placed her free hand on the glass door. She let the shower head fall. It swung violently, sprinkling the shower with water.

She inserted two fingers inside her pussy with her free hand and started to move them in and out.

"Oh my god, I'm cumming," Your cumming is (garbled).

"Cum inside (incoherent)."

Her orgasm spread throughout her body, causing her to

start shaking. She turned around in a full circle, her hand still supporting her against the shower wall.

I could see her fingers fluttering in and out as she parted her legs. Her cheeks were taut, clearly defining the divide.

"Daddy, you're so good,"

She shut off the water jets.

Her climax subsiding. It's best for me to leave. I pulled back.

I shut the door silently. I bided my time. I tapped.

May I? Hey, it's Daddy. How are you?"

Sure, allow me to take a moment to clean up."

As I waited, I sat on the bed.

She emerged from the restroom with a towel encircling her. The towel was short. The upper portion passed slightly above her areolas on her breasts. Her pussy was just barely covered by the bottom of the cloth. Now I had a full-fledged erection. It had pushed up and out against the baggy shorts after slipping out of my briefs. My cock's head and shaft were clearly visible.

It was increasing, so I had to divert my attention.

Have you spoken with Brandi?"

"Yes,"

"And how about...?""

She declined my gratitude. She's working until eight. She'll figure out how to handle a power loss at the apartment without your fucking assistance. It's a quotation. Not what I said.

"Well, at least we tried."

I sat silently.

"Dad," she said, indicating the door.

I apologize; I was thinking of Brandi.

My erection was still strong, so I needed to buy myself

some extra time. didn't really help when her towel undid when she sat next to me. Up close, her bare breasts are even more attractive. She re-encircled herself with the towel.

"Were you aware that your door was unlocked?""

"Oh no." I had to get ready quickly. I was unsure if you would have access to hot water for a shower in the coming days.

"April, a girl your age was raped and beaten in the building next door." Her door was still unlocked. If something were to happen to you, I would be devastated.'

"I apologize, Dad." Your genuine concern for me means a great deal.

She kissed me on the face and put her arms around me. She let go of her towel entirely throughout the process. Perhaps she noticed, but she didn't notice. Her bare breasts made contact with my chest as she gave me a hard hug.

She withdrew.

"I love you, Dad." I give you a lot of thought. I like how you treat me—just like your father would."

She then gave me a long, kiss on the lips. My chest was pressed up against her breasts.

My cock hurts to be near her hand, to feel her lips encircling her head, to be inside her pussy. I'm really, really horny.

I kissed her back, searching for her tongue. She gave me a strong tongue suck. I put my hands in front of us. She released her hold on me so I could softly caress her breasts, squeezing her nipples and pulling on them.

She ceased her kiss and leaned her cheek against mine, muttering.

Yes, Daddy. I'm very horny for you, take me. It's been a long time waiting for you.

With her hand sliding inside my shorts, she extracted my

pulsating erection.

"Daddy, it's so big and difficult." Could I intensify it more?"

With a nod. I said, "Sure, whatever you want to do with it."

She touched me gently. She moved between my legs, holding my cock in her hand. She swiftly undid my briefs and shorts and tossed them in the direction of the restroom.

Without warning, she kissed and sucked the top of my cock while holding the shaft's bottom with one hand and cupping my balls with the other.

I propped up my elbows and watched as my stepdaughter sucked on my penis.

The ideal setting for her tormenting was her enormous breasts hanging down and her nipples' stiff pillars protruding from the dark areolas. I was beyond the lighthearted banter.

Please put it in your mouth, April. Put your mouth around Daddy's arse.

She fulfilled my order. It felt so nice, my god. Her mouth, fully in touch with my head, and its warmth. This was incredibly excellent.

I'll make you cum in my mouth, Daddy. Then feel free to fuck me.

"Yes, please, proceed."

She moved sideways, encircling the base of the shaft and covering it with saliva all the way up to the head. Until she was satisfied, she repeated.

She moved up and down, gently at first, then picking up speed as she took hold of the head and then half of the shaft. That satisfying sensation waking up in my balls.

I've only ever experienced this amount of enthusiasm with Marilyn. The bonus this time is that my stepdaughter is lovingly licking my cock. Nothing compares to young women who have gone without sex, in my opinion.

It improved. She started to go crazy over my cock, sucking on my balls one at a time and drawing them out as far as the sack would allow, pulling back, and rubbing my cock across her face. Repeat. mumbling about how much she enjoyed sucking my cock and how much she needed it. She adored her father's manhood.

She hesitated, gripped the shaft's base, lowered the head all the way to the top of her hand, and then slowly raised it again. She withdrew her hand, kissed my pubic hair, and continued to move her head back and forth while maintaining touch with my pelvis.

She stayed bottomed out on my huge shaft and met my gaze. She was really, really great!

Time had come.

She kept retreating all the way off and then returning to the bottom. I was completely out of control. I could feel my balls tingling and my mind racing with ideas. I was so aroused.

She picked up on my thoughts and quickened the tempo, taking my fucking cock in so many times I could lose count. I could only see stars, and nothing else could possibly fit through the tight opening left by her mouth on my cock. With my head out of control, my orgasm was accelerating to its maximum pace.

"April, April, I'm cumming, baby."

She withdrew and gave him a sharp push. It didn't take long because I was so far along. My peak gushing sperm out over her cheek, forehead, right eye, and hair. She resumed her activity, limiting the throbbing torrents to her lips and throat. It seemed as though I had been there for minutes, with each drip heightening the pleasure of a fulfilling orgasm. a climax brought on by my stepdaughter, my daughter.

My stepdaughter just gave me the blowjob of the century! How am I acting?

April gave my thigh a tap. That jolted me out of my daydream.

She gestured to her parted lips. filled of my white belongings. Shutting her mouth, she took a swallow.

"It's nice, and I want more." It's time to screw me, dad.

Pulling me off the bed, she lay with her legs wide apart and her moisture shining on her pussy.

"Daddy, hurry up before it goes limp."

I stretched between her thighs. I repeatedly touched her clit after rubbing my moist cock across her lips.

I'm fucked, dad. I looked after you, so screw me.

I gently placed the tip in between the labia and pulled the lips inward. She grasped my cheeks and dragged me down, causing me to surrender completely to her. Her pubic hair is now tangled in mine.

"Yeah, that feels great, Daddy. Fuck me hard now." Grab me, Daddy. More of your cum, please.

Someone was shouting something and banging on the door. We said nothing. I could hear him now 'answering the door' and stating he was the manager.

sounded grave. I left April behind. I forced my hard on between my legs and pushed it inside my briefs before pulling up my work out shorts.

As I approached the door, he continued to bang on it.

I took it open.

'April is not you.'

Very perceptive. I'm her father.

"No, I've met her father; he frequently pays her a visit." He got his own key from me.

That's interesting, all right.

I apologize; I'm her stepdad.

Jennifer revealed the cause for the divorce after a year of marriage. On her eighteenth birthday, April's ex had made her have sex with him. both verbal and sexual.

Was April okay with it, perhaps? Perhaps that was not me in the bathtub masturbating, but rather the genuine 'Daddy'. Does she want me to be her biological father? Have regular sex with her?

I am alerting everyone to the fact that we are without a generator. that it is their own risk to remain. In addition, the hill leading out of the complex has gotten worse due to ice. A number of autos are trapped.

Is your SUV that one?He gestured toward my nearby parked automobile.

"Yes,"

Will you be traveling somewhere else in April?"

"Yes,"

'I would leave right now if I were you.'

That is our strategy. I appreciate the update.

He gave me a glance.

I apologize, but are you her stepfather? If you understand what I mean, she receives a lot of visitors. me as well.

He grinned. Understandably, he was concerned about her.

I shut the door behind him. I pivoted to return to the bedroom. April gestured to me with her finger as she stood in the doorway.

"Go on, Dad." Get back in bed. I'm still drenched.

We have to go, April. The manager issued a warning regarding the difficulty of leaving the property. We have the entire evening to...

"To screw me? Sure, Come on, let's go.

"April, I'll be waiting for you in the living room."

I settled myself on the sofa. My frustration is finally fading.

What happens next? We may spend a night or two alone together, at the very least. No way can I fuck her. I've gone so far as to let her deceive me, which was fantastic. Far superior to her mother.

Who can say? If Brandi could come along, it would be great and beneficial. April and her may have their own space. My part is done. When we return home, I'll give her a try.

In any case, I can't make matters worse by allowing my sexual desires for women—girls April's age—to rule my life. Be resilient! I told them not to mess this marriage up in my good voice.

All I have to do is be strong. I adore Jennifer very much.

April appeared fully clothed, sporting pants and a modest top. I feared she could come after me once more. Actually, I was hoping she would. She was prepared for her stepdad to fuck her as she was hot and wet.

With her was a bag.

"April, grab your snowboard." For the frigid weather, you could need everything but the skis.

"That's what's in the bag, got it."

A brief period of silence.

"Dad, is there anything we should discuss?"

April, we don't do that. While the going is good, let's get started.

We were able to take the slope. Four vehicles stranded on the hill. Though I was tempted to assist, I refrained. April and I are going to a bed.

We arrived at my driveway to find it slightly raining and 25 degrees outside. All the streets and parked automobiles had ice on them. How quickly things transpired is amazing. I'm glad we can stay put and wait things out. We should always have power and had an abundance of food and beverages.

Wordlessly, April made her way to her former room. I switched to the regional station. It was actually a woman weatherman, and my favorite. She had placed second in Miss America and served as Miss Florida. She is someone I could watch day and night.

In other words, avoid going outside if it's not necessary. Things are becoming worse very quickly. The bridges have frozen over already. Main streets are becoming harder for street crews to maintain open. Hills and side streets will be in disarray.

"The temperature has already dropped into the teens two hundred miles northward." a touch below zero and to the north.

"The governor is requesting that you use less electricity." Stress is already evident in the grid. The ice is building quickly and is causing power wires to droop. Another paper covered the issue of frozen valves at natural gas pumping stations. The plants that produce electricity are fed by these pumping stations. These plants could suddenly stop working.

"This is the worst weather event I have seen in ten years of reporting," the viewer said. Kindly consider this carefully. Get ready for a blackout. Stock up on extra blankets and batteries for your gadgets and lamps. If you use your car to charge anything, make sure the exhaust is directed toward a ventilated area.

Make sure you have food that you can prepare without using any electricity. Keep bottled water on hand in case the water supply is affected.

Whoa! I changed to a different local channel. The same dire cautions.

And so did The Weather Channel. Naturally, there are already reports from people who live close to our house and the ice-covered streets. The reporter was surrounded by sliding cars and trucks. Perilous!

April came to watch the news with me.

"Dad, this is frightful." I'm happy to be here with you.

She gave my arm a hug. She shot me that "let's fuck, kiss me" expression. I disregarded it. Her cell rang.

"Brandi, how are you?""

April paid close attention. She gave the phone to me.

"She must speak with you."

"Brandi, are you alright?""

My automobile won't start, Dad. The only vehicle remaining in the lot is mine. Dad ... Dad ... I am... I...

"Brandi, I am en route." Hold onto your automobile. I'll get there as quickly as I can.

"Thanks, Dad. I apologize for treating you like such a bitch." However, I think you hurt me more than you hurt Mom. I felt envious.

Envious?

"Brandi, when I get you here, we can talk it through." Hold on tight.

"Yes, I do love you, Dad."

"To Brandi, I love you."

I ended the call.

"April, come stay with me while I fetch Brandi."

No, I'll be joining you. I'm not going to be by myself here. Suppose there is a power outage. I have no idea how to turn on the generator.

"April, it turns on by itself the moment it senses that our house is without power."

"Well, that's fantastic, but I'm still coming,"

Alright. Put on your ski gear. We could have to backtrack, who knows.

Nothing I hadn't seen previously when I lived up north, but

it was a terrifying drive. I generally used my two wheels to navigate the grass next to the icy street. strong grip on the grass. We drove by a number of abandoned cars.

We arrived at the outside parking area, where there was no grass to enjoy.

We approached Brandi's car—the only one in the lot—very slowly, moving forward without making any abrupt movements and braking very gradually. We were getting near, so I flashed my brights to let her know. I pulled up behind her vehicle.

As soon as she was outside, she slid and fell on the ground. She remained still.

"April, hold on to the car while I help Brandi."

I skied like a cross-country skier out on the ice, sliding my feet forward and backward until I reached Brandi without falling.

She was lifeless, laying flat on the ice. Her black lace

panties were visible since her short skirt had ridden up on her lips. I enjoy them.

"Brandi, are you alright?""

Yes, Dad, I just can't bring myself to get up.

Her heels were quite high! It makes sense why she slipped. It was 80 degrees in the morning, yet she was dressed inappropriately for the weather—short skirt and low-cut shirt!

I quickly thought. I helped her get into the car by pulling her to the side and opening the door.

You won't have to walk at all if you stay here while I park the car.

I slipped once, but I made it to the car without falling. I carefully shifted the car forward so that my back door opened in front of hers. She was able to enter my automobile with the help of the two doors working as a fence. It succeeded. After she shut the door.

"Dad, I'm freezing." My feet are quite cold. I am shivering.

"It's here, the heat is intense. Please place your feet beneath my seat; there is a vent there."

"Oh my god, that feels amazing." Without you, Dad, I don't know what I would have done. You are my hero.

We're still not at home. Here we proceed.

I closed her car door by pushing it through my window.

The same terrifying, white-knuckle drive home. However, we survived.

Power remains on. For now, at least, that's good.

The house was getting too cold for the HVAC to handle. It was constantly operating.

Brandi was given the task of searching Jennifer's wardrobe for something warm to wear. She emerged wearing loose-fitting fleece workout trousers and a hooded sweater. Fuzzy slippers and socks finished the unattractive ensemble.

April wore one of my flannel shirts, unbuttoned all the way down to her breasts. Her white underwear was hardly covered by her tail. I was shocked to see that she was wearing underwear.

I was wearing my baggy flannel pajamas now. Pleasant, cozy, and toasty.

To commemorate our enjoyable trip, we made the decision to open a bottle of wine. That quickly emptied. As I was preparing dinner, I cracked open another.

The second bottle was empty, and the third was opened for dinnertime use.

The lights blinked but remained on as we were finishing the third bottle and dinner.

"Dad, will the power go out for us?""Brandi enquired."

The generator will start if we do. Just the internet, the refrigerator, the heat, and a few lights are powered by it. I gave it a try today, and it functions.

We have an abundance of flashlights, and some of the lights have built-in battery-operated bulbs. We are thus OK.

"Dad, how are the fireplaces doing?" Shall we switch on the one in the living room? Maybe help us get warmer.

I also gave it a try. It needs a part that no one has on hand and isn't working.

The main bedroom has a fireplace, right?April inquired, aware that she was acting in Brandi's best interest.

That functions.

"That's great, we can all spend the night in there."

April gave me a wink and moved two fingers in and out of her lips, all while keeping Brandi from seeing her.

You two will sleep there if that's all we have. I'll be fine in the visitor bedroom.

April shot me a dejected glance and pulled out her bottom lip in response.

Would you mind spending the night with me, Brandi?April enquired.

Indeed.

After clearing away our dinnerware, we took a seat on the sofa. A daughter beside me on both sides.

With her shirt blown open and her breasts fully exposed, April wrapped her arm around me. The nipple is firm already. What did she intend to do?

We watched one of my favorite movies, Home Alone. It was Brandi's turn, and she picked a sweet and humorous romantic comedy. It's April now...

She found the adult streaming service by navigating. Lots of useful stuff there. Soft pornography was her choice. Of course.

April put one hand on my thigh and continued to encircle

me with her arm. A lightning strike grazed my balls. I remembered the amazing blowjob she had given me. A flaming erection.

The characters—Mom, Dad, and the twin daughters—developed from the film's innocent beginnings. on a Bahamas vacation. That looked so warm!

Then things began to go wrong. In the bedroom, mom and daughter engaged in a sensual lesbian sexual encounter. You could tell that Mom was working her pussy between her daughter's legs even in the blurry and hurried photos.

In a cabana, father and daughter. Daughter undies her father and pulls down his shorts. A fleeting glimpse of his erection. Next shot: rear view of the camera with his daughter nestled between his knees. Without getting a clear sight, you could tell that she was massaging his balls and licking his cock. God, I was starting to grow tough again, remembering April's blowjob.

Rewind to the mother and daughter. Even without a direct view from the camera, you can see they were scissoring. I caught a glimpse of Brandi reaching into her sweatpants with her hand.

April reached over to touch my erection. I didn't try to reject or hide it. That much was clear to her.

The father takes hold of his daughter's back and yanks it down into a hard chokehold. Her head moves in sync with his bucking up and down.

He yells, "Oh my god, baby, I'm cumming!""

I really wanted April to take out my cock and follow suit, but I can't right now because of Brandi. I gave Brandi a look. With her hands on her mother's breasts, her fingers playing with her nipples, she was fixated on the following scene. They displayed everything.

While gripping her breasts, Brandi started finger fucking her pussy.

Next, though... After a few blinks, the lights went off, leaving the room completely dark.

"Generator, please come on!I uttered.

April the mischievous one exploited the darkness. She took my cock out and stroked the shaft with her lips wrapped around it. After seeing the mild porn, I was really hard. She needs to stop or I'll explode into her mouth once again because I was hot.

Brandi was grumbling. Into her, fingers deep.

At last, the generator started up. That wasn't supposed to take so long. There was a problem. I must investigate it.

April took a swift step back and tried to place my extremely firm erection back where she found it. It was failing her. I intervened just in time to prevent Brandi from penetrating her pussy.

"I apologize to all." I went overboard. I lost control because that was so fucking erotic. My last date was six months ago. I was unable to. Breathlessly, "I couldn't stop myself," said Brandi.

She turned to face April and me.

"Dad, it appears that you were having fun too." Examine the dimensions of your... your climax. Mom must miss it.

April, did you feel the same way?"

Oh, I see. I'm incredibly turned on after seeing Dad's erection as well.

I needed to leave that place.

Hello, I need to examine the generator. It ought to have manifested earlier. I have to stop it in order to do it. The lights will turn on if there is street electricity; if not, they will turn on using batteries.

Got it, dad, need our assistance?April enquired.

I don't believe so. I must change so that I can go outside.

I bundled up and walked through the garage to the

generator in the backyard. The drive was particularly slick. To reach the generator, I grabbed onto the wall.

The danger light was on, but it was running. I opened the control application. A discovered gas leak in the generator was the reason for the notice. It is advised to turn off the generator's gas supply. Fuck! Not a single other hint about how to find the leak. Something likely cracked after freezing.

To let it run and incur the risk of an explosion was the other alternative.

I turned it off. The lights on the driveway flickered on and off. Yes, the street light is back on. For now, though.

I told the girls the news when I got back inside the house.

Dad and I had a conversation. We believe it would be better for us to all sleep together in the master bedroom when it comes time to go to bed if we lose electricity once more. We tested the fireplace there, and it functions properly. Daddy has to be kept warm all night. You are aware in case repairs are necessary.

I was yelling to myself within, "Yes, let's do it." Fantastic concept. Now let's head to bed! However, I said instead...

"Thank you, but the guest bedroom will suffice for me."

"Well, that's what we anticipated you saying," Brandi remarked.

However, we have chosen to share a bed with you in any bedroom, so let's use the master. We are your daughters, so hurry up, Dad. "It's not like you'll be sharing a bed with two Marilyns," Brandi continued, giving me a sardonic look.

I'm sure April put her through this. I have no idea why she believes that we can have sex in the bed with Brandi there.

"All right, you two can go to bed with me."

April nodded to Brandi after giving me a wink. What was meant by that?

"Joy!" All we need now is the ability to leave and stay outside, Brandi remarked.

They were winning now. One more curve and turn.

"Dad, how about we go to some card games?" As we used to when I was younger,' inquired Brandi.

"I think that's a really good idea." At last, something typical to perform.

"April has a clever card game idea."

Oh no.

Yeah. April remarked, "Daddy, let's play strip poker."

Are you kidding me, please? Are you cool with that, Brandi?"

Indeed, it is preferable than playing for cash. It's only a game, Dad, come on, it will be more entertaining that way.

"There's nothing to be concerned about," Brandi smiled.

"Go on, Dad." We either play now or head straight to bed.

Isn't it too early?April grinned.

Although I knew Brandi would be fine with it, I answered yes even though I shouldn't have. What's happened to her? She had already claimed to be envious when we discussed my infidelity with Marilyn.

"Alright, but Brandi, you need to respond to this question first."

"Shot!""

"What made you feel envious of Marilyn and me?""

With a flush, she turned to face her hands.

It is awkward to bring up the subject.

April chimed in, "I know! She requested that you fuck her.

Brandi nodded when I looked at her.

Is that the reason you have been so irate with me, Brandi?"

She gave another nod.

"I had no idea." Nothing I ever seen led me to believe that.

Yes, you did, but you disregarded all of my hints to pique your curiosity. Do you recall asking you to bring me a towel while I had a shower? Do you recall that time we watched a movie and I was clad in nothing but a V-neck T-shirt and no underwear? You definitely saw my pussy.

And we slept in the same bed in the hotel when you went me to see a university, and I cuddled with you all night long? You definitely had an erection, I think.

She was accurate. I was banging Marilyn like mad at the time, but I did recall all that. I repressed my desire for Brandi and remained strong. Why did I just tell her a lie?

"Okay, April, deal."

This may be enjoyable. The thought of a threesome with my girls was starting to appeal to me.

"Daddy, there can't be more than two outfits for each of us." Take him down to his underwear and pants, Brandi. Keep us waiting for the huge, big prize, please.

Brandi stepped behind the chair and me. She grabbed my sweatshirt around the waist and tugged it up. She reached across my chest to the cold gear shirt I was wearing from behind me. She lifted it and removed it.

Rather than going back to her seat, she wrapped her fingers around my nipples, giving them a firm squeeze. April shifted to sit next to me while she was working. She kissed me on the lips, softly moving my head up and to the right. The plan was succeeding if its goal was to hurt me badly.

They went back to their places at the tiny kitchen table, one beside the other.

"These are the rules, Daddy." Our game is five-car poker. Up to two may be discarded, and replacements may be drawn.

"Low hand strips, high hand wins." But ... The article of clothing is taken off by the high hand. The middle hand is obviously watching.

"Everyone in a tie chooses one card until the highest card wins if there is a tie."

"The loser must carry out the winner's instructions if they run out of clothes."

"I see now. "Good luck to you both." I find the stripping rule amusing.

April lost the first hand, and Brandi won. April relocated to take Brandi's place. She undid her underwear by pulling it down. April turned to face me, her shirt up so I could see her pussy. She separated her legs. She parted the labia with her fingertips.

"This is yours tonight, Daddy."

Second, I was defeated once more by Brandi! In front of her, I stood. She untied my pants' tie. She slipped her fingers inside my briefs' side pockets. She took them down one by one. My briefs were also being dragged down by the movement. April took note.

"Brandi, you cannot take two pieces with a single winning hand!"

"I apologize, but his briefs are too tight."

She took up my briefs again. I was going nuts over this!

Third hand: Brandi won once more, and I lost! I stepped in front of her, my head dripping and discoloring the white briefs as I pushed them to their breaking point.

April knelt between us, her cheek on my protruding phallus. Her lips were being licked.

Slowly, Brandi peeled my briefs all the way down to my shaft.

There was a phone call.

"That's mine," declared Brandi. This is Mom's ring. I had to respond.

She got to her feet and went to get her phone off the counter.

April asserted, "I can defeat him."

She stepped in front of me quite swiftly.

"No!" April, stop! Take a seat now!remarked Brandi.

April got up and sank back into her chair, sulking like a six-year-old whose favorite toy was taken away from her for misbehaving. Her arms were crossed.

"Hey, mom."

'Put her on speaker,' I muttered. Yes, she did.

"Brandi, what's up?" We just contacted the office, but nobody answered.

"I'm with Dad, Mom."

"Papa!" You are with him, but why?"

I called him for assistance because my car wouldn't start. He went out on the ice to get me. He is excellent.

You need to have given Rocco a call. He could have been useful.

"You know I detest his egotistical guts, Mom?" I am not sure what you perceive in him. Somehow, he must have a large cock.

"Brandy!" You dare me! He has shown us kindness.

None of it. Talk to Dad here.

I moved to her chair and stood in front of her, my erection forcing the halfway down briefs out even farther. She gave the phone to me. It was my.

My cock protruded straight out of my briefs, inches from her lips, as she quickly yanked them down. April scurried to get back on her knees between us. Brandi kissed the top of her head.

All I could manage to say as I watched Brandi put my cock in her mouth was "hi."

You are her hero, then.

I disagree with that. She despises my insides.

April applied saliva by wrapping her lips longitudinally over the shaft and pushing it up and down toward the head. It took me off guard.

God, I exclaimed.

"What?" What is the issue?"

Brandi was now midway through my shaft.

"The lighting flickered."

Yes. I do appreciate you saving her, though. Rocco will take her to stay with us in his Hummer if the weather improves in the morning.

Alright, it makes sense. When he arrives, ask him to call.

"All right, give Brandi another call."

Brandi was jumping up and down on me in a hurry. April had moved in to have sex with my privates.

* She... She was... She used the restroom.

Tell her I adore her and am so excited to see her, okay?

And once again, I appreciate your assistance. Perhaps you're not really such a jerk.

She let out a big laugh.

Bye, I uttered.

I was being reserved since I really wanted to cum in Brandi's mouth.

"Girls, let's get over our games," I remarked. Come with me to bed.

Yeah! They all said, "Agreed."

I made my rules in the bedroom.

"I will control you now, as you have been controlling me."

You'll comply with all I ask of you. One sexual act per person under supervision is the limit. Do you think that's okay?"

Brandi: "Yes, Daddy, please boss me around. I'm ready."

I'm prepared to be your sexy, cocksucking harlot.

April, it's fantastic! Is it possible for us to alternate taking charge during the evening?"

Indeed. Come on in, April.

She moved forward and took a position just in front of me. I undid the rest of her shirt's buttons. I locked her arms behind her by pulling it back down. Her nipples were firm and her breasts protruded.

Nice, the way it looks good. With your head dangling over the edge, lie on your back.

She hastily assumed her position, taking off her clothes. She immediately massaged her clit while playing with her pussy. her nipples with the other hand.

"Brandy!""

In front of me stood she. I took down her panties and sweatpants and repeatedly tapped her clit. I removed her hoodie. I spun her in circles. My penis was wedged between her legs. I touched her nipples and toyed with them. She attempted to insert my cock into her crotch.

"Brandi, recline as if it were April."

She complied.

I crept forward, stroking my cock, approaching the edge of the bed. They were staring at my incredibly strong erection. The veins emerging from the thin shaft skin layer.

"Open your mouths wide, both of you."

April's lips opened to receive my cock first, and she tore it off, tonguing the head and squeezing harder to get more. I made my exit.

I quickly pushed it in farther as I moved to Brandi. I pulled out once more, but she locked my lips on the shaft.

I made multiple trips back and forth to give them a taste of what was to come.

"First, who needs Daddy's cock?""

"Me, I was going to get it, then my phone rang," was

Brandi's prompt response.

"Oh, that's too bad you got a call; I should get it," April replied.

I was with April earlier, so...

"Brandi, let me in."

I got down on my hands and knees and carefully put my cock in her mouth. her arms parallel to her body. Her firm, protruding breasts nippled.

I pressed closer. She handled it quite nicely. I maintained my cock posture. I extended my arms and reached down to her ass. I gave her a tight kiss and caressed her lips together. She bucked up demanding more touch, saying she liked it. In addition, she attempted to take more of my cock, but I resisted.

I pushed two fingers all the way in, causing my hand to collide with her clit as I did so.

I pressed down on it. Her lips was stuffed as she tried to

sigh.

I continued to press my cock in; she was taking it well. a little bit more. Excellent nonetheless. The head came into contact with her throat's opening a little farther. Pushing the head a little further into her throat. She shoved me away out of instinct and choked. Allowing her.

She signaled for me to go.

With my pubic hair lying on her lips and chin, I pushed it all the way in. Not to choke. I didn't move back at all, holding it deep inside. In her throat, just below her chin, I could see the silhouette of a head. I gave it a pat. So I gave it a squeeze. I was aware of it.

She gave the signal to get out. then to carry on.

Once more, I went all the way down, wriggling my cock back and forth and smacking her nose with my balls. She tugged at her nipples till the flesh gave way.

I completely withdrew and relocated to April.

No, Daddy. Please return. Please fuck my face.

I disregarded her.

April, open your legs and show me your pussy while you're on all fours. Move under her pussy on your back, Brandi.

I reddened April's tense cheeks with a slap. I used my fingers to separate her lips and reveal my cock's entry site through the pink skin. I spat on it multiple times, distributing the saliva with my fingers.

I got up.

"Brandi, spritz me."

She took hold of my cock and brought it to her lips, licking the head and shaft before partially inhaling it. I could sense the moisture. I prepared.

I pushed the moist lips apart as I inserted the tip. In an attempt to get more of my cock within her, she shifted back. Abruptly, I completely moved in, pressing my bottom against her dripping pussy.

Yes, Daddy, I see. That's my desire. I have been waiting all night for it.

Brandi approached and tried to put her tongue in my balls.

I started out cautiously and worked my way back in. I accelerated the speed. Enjoying the voyage so much, April put her head down to rest on the bed.

"Brandi, give it to her."

She tapped, massaged, and pinched her clit.

"Oh my..." Oh my gosh. Daddy, give me more fucks. I can feel my orgasm beginning.

Rather, I withdrew and showed Brandi my wet erection, which she accepted and repeatedly sucked on.

I'm back inside April, giving her a hard thump. My balls were tingling, and I couldn't resist the need to let go.

"Oh my god, I'm cumming,"

She breathed heavily, shivering and moaned every now and then. I continued to fuck.

"Daddy, fuck, fuck, fuck."

She shifted in front of me, intensifying the force of my thrusts against her. I was at my breaking point. I growled with delight at cumming in my stepdaughter, but I stopped thrusting and released my load, one spurt at a time, deep inside her.

I was through. Little strings of cum were hanging from my head when I pulled my cum-soaked cock out.

Brandi took a step forward and grabbed my cock's cum. She moved under April right away.

We were pushing the cum out in April. Seeing my white stuff trickle out and land in Brandi's eager mouth was a lovely sight. April's pussy had some cum left on it, so Brandi moved in to lick it.

On the bed's edge, they took a seat. Brandi's lips and chin

are slightly moistened.

April kissed her openly and lowered her head. Brandi poured all of the sperm into her lips. They licked and kissed one another's faces. Full transfer achieved. With a white mouth, April opened up.

Again, they switched, and Brandi's mouth got full. She took it all in.

My turn, Daddy. It's my turn to be screwed. Says Brandi.

Do not forget, one per person. It will be your turn to take the reins. Fantastic! I have a sultry notion of how I would like to be fucked by you. Is it your responsibility to complete it? "Yes." "It's my turn to take charge." "Yes."

Her phone rang once more. Why does she always seem to receive calls at inconvenient times?

Her eyes regarded it inquisitively.

Marilyn is here. What makes her calling me?

With a shrug, I released it. She and I haven't spoken for a full year.

"Marilyn, how are you?" I asked, not knowing who else to call. My parents are in Cancun. I'm sitting in my cold, dark house and I was hoping you might know someone who could help. My boyfriend is, well, he's no longer my boyfriend. Someone similar to your father.

I took the phone from Brandi.

It's me, Marilyn!

Are you able to come get me? You own a generator, I seem to recall.

Though it's not working, I do. We still have electricity, though.' Oh, would you please come get me? You have my eternal gratitude. I regret not being able to have sex with you.

April had four fingers up when I turned to look at her. Then she created a circle with her index finger and thumb. With her other hand, she moved two fingers moving in and out of the circle and then shoved them deep into her mouth.

I get it.

'Hold on.'

I muted the phone.

'Would you be OK with that? I mean going to get her.'

April had a huge grin.

Sure! A foursome!' 'Dad, could you handle the three of us?' Brandi asked with a knowing smile.

'Yep, she will fit right in if you know what I mean. Remember, I am in control. I hope she likes sex games.'

'She better. Let's go!' shouted April.

Mute off.

'Marilyn, we are on our way. Prepare yourself to have a great time.'

She said, 'I am wet just thinking about sucking your big,

thick cock again.'

'Bye!'

All I can say is, I hope this storm never ends.

Acknowledgments

The Glory of this book's success goes to God Almighty and my beautiful Family, Fans, Readers & well-wishers, Customers, and Friends for their endless support and encouragement.

About The Author

I've spent nearly a decade penning romantic novels. As a passionate writer of erotica, I craft dark, romantic erotica. Anime Naked Truth Se of Sacred Sexuality: Forbidden Seducing Short Stories of an Erotica Nude Sexy Girl Poster. Alongside Erotic Mystery Fiction, Victorian Erotica Sex, Black & African American Erotica, Euthanasia, Daddy Teaching, Forced Domination, Alpha Monster Cuckold, and BDSM for Adults, there's an Erotic Fiction in Kinky Family. I write dark, sensual romance because I adore the power of darkness and everything that it entails. Romance novels have always been my favorite kind of books, and now I'm writing them. The idea that you will like reading and enjoying my fiction as much as I enjoy pushing the frontiers of sexual pleasure in my writing thrills me more than anything else.